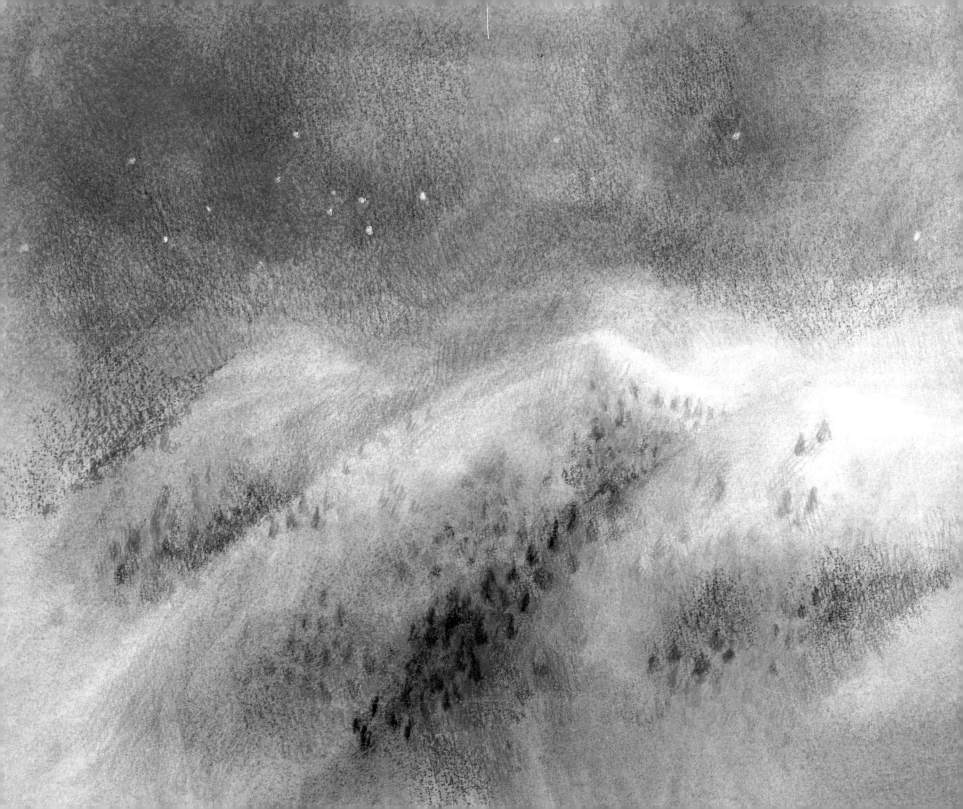

Peter William Butterblow

and other little folk

A picture book by Bettina Stietencron
With verses by C J Moore
based on German poems by Marianne Garff, Alfred Baur and Hedwig Diestel

Floris Books

Here's a little climbing team
struggling up beside the stream;
trudging with true grit and hope,
they brave the mist and rocky slope.

The one in front is Baldigrand,
leader of the little band,
with the lantern in his hand.
Then there comes old Patterpout
who is, I must say, rather stout
but sturdily keeps stepping out.
Behind him, kind Gazumptitum
is waiting for his tiny chum,
young Peter William Butterblow
who is really *very* slow.

Just now the going's rough and hard;
they press on grimly, yard by yard.
But once they reach the mountain top
how they'll run and skip and hop!

So quietly they stand, hour after hour,
in the woods, listening ...
What do they hear? Tell me, pray,
what is there to listen to all day?

They hear the rustle of mice and voles
scurrying to and from their holes;
they hear the murmuring of bees
fetching nectar from the trees;
they hear the green woodpecker's drumming,
the busy insects' endless humming;
they hear the fox so softly slinking;
a mother bird's alarm chink-chinking.

At last a gentle evening breeze
comes to stir their peaceful ease;
and then they hear the clumping feet
of hungry gnomes off home to eat.

Trit-trot, trit-trot,
here's a little fellow
walking through the woods
with his sack upon his back,
in the dewy dawn light.
Trit-trot, trit-trot.

The cuckoo calls: "cuck-oo, cuck-oo!"
The chattering squirrels hide from view;
so does the deer, afraid and shy.
But see, the little mouse
peeps from her tiny house
to see who's walking by.

Trit-trot, trit-trot,
here's a little fellow
walking through the woods
with his sack upon his back,
in the dewy dawn light.
Trit-trot, trit-trot.

Old gnome Trustytrout
lives behind the stove.
Every night he sallies out
from his warm alcove.

Once he's shut the kitchen door,
he scrubs the table, sweeps the floor,
chops the kindling, fetches coals,
dries the dishes, plates and bowls.

Working as quietly as he can,
he stokes the fire and turns the pan,
then humming softly to himself
he tidies up the cupboard shelf.

At last when all is neatly stored
it's time for his usual reward:
nuts with syrup and, of course,
porridge oats with apple sauce.

Next a tasty bit of cheese
goes rather well. Then, if you please,
a large slice of that almond cake
which the family loves to bake.

Then with much "Mmm!" and "Yummy-yummy!"
licking lips and rubbing tummy,
the old gnome curls up in a heap
and very soon is fast asleep.

Under the bright summer sun
what could be more fun
than to go searching far and wide
all along the warm hillside?

How soon the summer day will pass
with hunting through the hazy grass.
Take your jug or pot or cup:
don't stop until you fill it up.

And why do we spend these happy hours
searching amongst the meadow flowers?
To find wild strawberries ripe and red
for a supper snack with milk and bread.

Sometimes at night upon the stair
little sounds disturb the air:
tiny slippers flip-flop-flapping,
tiny hands clap-clap-clapping,
a little bell ring-ring-ringing,
a little voice sing-sing-singing.

Who's that wandering through our house?
Is it a child? Is it a mouse?
Who's that roaming about our home?
I do believe — it's a little gnome!

Heaving-oh and humping-oh, homeward bound they track,
each one with a precious load on his little back,
each one with a basketful, coming two by two:
quartz, agate and crystals, jewels of every hue;
nuggets from the quarry, gold dust from the stream,
silver from the mountain's heart — a poor man's dream!
All this wealth and riches will secretly be stored
where nobody will ever find the gnomes' treasure-hoard!

All night long on the mountainside
the gnomes dance and play
under the silent circling stars,
from the first fall of eventide
till the bright break of day.

Round and round and round they whirl
in their joyful throng;
and down in the valley town below
the dreams of a sleeping boy or girl
may echo with a faint, far off song.

First published in German as *Nachts am Berge tanzen die Zwerge*
© 1991 by Verlag Engel & Seefels, Stuttgart
English version © 1991 by Floris Books, 15 Harrison Gardens, Edinburgh
British Library CIP Data available   ISBN 0-86315-125-6
Third printing 2000   Printed in Belgium